FAUST:
A Tale of La Negrita,
The Patron Saint of Costa Rica

________________________________

By

Walter Joseph Schenck, Jr.

FAUST: A Tale of La Negrita,
The Patron Saint of Costa Rica
Copyright © 2020
by Walter Joseph Schenck, Jr.

All rights reserved. No part of this book may be used or reproduced by any means, graphic, electronic, or mechanical, including photocopying, recording, taping, or by any informational storage retrieval system without the written permission of the writer except in the case of brief quotations embodied in critical articles and reviews.

This stage play is a work of fiction. Names, characters, places, and incidents either are the product of the author's imagination or are used fictitiously, and any resemblance to actual persons, living or dead, events, or locales is entirely coincidental.

Caution: This script is provided for reading purposes only. Professionals and amateurs are hereby advised that this stage play, *FAUST: A Tale of La Negrita, The Patron Saint of Costa Rica* is subject to royalty. The stage play, *FAUST: A Tale of La Negrita, The Patron Saint of Costa Rica,* is fully protected under the laws of the United States of America, South Africa, the British Empire, including the Dominion of Canada, and all other countries of the Copyright Union. All rights, including but not limited to professional, amateur, film, radio, and all other media (including use on the World Wide Web) and the rights of translation into foreign languages are strictly reserved; and any unauthorized use of the material may subject the user to any and all applicable civil and criminal penalties.

No performance of any kind may be given unless a license has been obtained.

Publication and/or purchase of this play does not permit its availability for performance.

For any information about royalties or to apply for a performance license, please email:

Walter_schenck@comcast.net

ISBN: 9798569113545
Imprint: Independently published

Printed in the United States of America
In Courier 12 point

*DEDICATED TO*

All Vietnam Veterans

And, as always,

To my wife,
Molly Schenck

Concerning the Stage Play Formatting

As I am a Professional member of the Dramatists Guild of America, I asked the organization quite a few questions concerning the proper formatting of a stage play, especially in consideration of their two format offerings in Final Draft. After several ideas were explored, I decided to create a universal format applicable to all stage plays, and entitled it *How to Correctly Format A Stage Play.*

The formatting in this version will seem strange at first glance, but it is mathematically precise, obeying the strict parameters set out in the published guideline. This formula meets the approval of the Dramatist Guide.

Briefly:

1. Fonts must always be Courier New 12 point font while the page should be 8.5 inches by 11 inches, or, letter size.

2. Dialogue begins at 1.5 inches from the left edge without indentation.

    a. Right hand side of the dialogue will be jagged, unless the author intentionally justifies the text. The jagged formatting is to honor the historic usage of manual typewriter. If the author justifies the dialogue, and there are over two paragraphs, each paragraph should be indented .25 inch.

3. Character names are to be centered in caps with .5 inch offset (to emphasize the preceding action on the second line), and centered.

    a. A character's name should never end the page, but rather, should be placed on the top of the following page.
    b. The character's moods, actions, and directions should be enclosed inside parentheses centered directly underneath the character's name.

CHARACTER'S NAME CAPS with .05 inch offset
(Parentheses action line is centered)

4. CAST OF CHARACTERS offset by 4.5 inches from left
   edge of the paper with jagged text on right-hand
   side. Can be either justified or not.

5. Exit and enter directions on the extreme right side
   with character names in caps, enclosed in
   parentheses, 5.5 inches from the left margin.

                                        (Exit THOMAS)

                                        (Enter WIFE)

6. Stage Directions and Dialogue instructions are
   properly placed 3 inches from left margin with a
   maximum range of 6.5 inches, rendered within
   parenthesis, jagged right edge.

            (For example: this is how to
             perform the method, with jagged
             right hand.)

7. Character orphans. Do not end the page with a
   character's name. Create a new page with the name
   centered and offset by .5 inches on the top of the
   next page.

8. ACTs and Scenes are placed 5 inches from the left
   margin. ACTS is in caps while Scenes is rendered in
   caps and lowercase.

9. SETTING begins at left margin with location offset
   at 4.5 inches.

10. Dialogue interruption occurs when a person enters
    or exits during the speech. When the original
    speaker continues his dialogue, place the same

character's name in the center of the page with the
[CON'T] designation after the comma.

While a screenplay utilizes (), a stage play uses [].

                    THOMAS
Goodbye.

                                        (Exit WIFE)

                                        (Enter SON)

                    THOMAS, [CON'T]
How are you?

                        **

              Special Note:
Please do not confuse the dialogue interruption of the
stage play with the action line of a screenplay.

I also discussed with the Dramatist Guild the usage of
MORE whenever the dialogue shifts from one page to the
next and they assured the placement of MORE is only
used by the screenplay format. The usage of
"Continued" is not incorporated in either format of
FINAL DRAFT.

<u>CAST OF CHARACTERS</u>

FAUST:   Hispanic. Retired. Dying from blood cancer. Highly decorated officer during the Vietnam War.

YOUNG FAUST:   Faust as a youth, reenacting his memories.

MARGARET:   Faust's wife.

WAGNER:   Faust's best friend. They fought together in Vietnam. After Wagner's death from cancer, he returns as a ghost transporting him back in time where the Battle of An Loc is reenacted.

YOUNG WAGNER:   Wagner as a youth, reenacting his memories.

RACHAEL:   A mysterious neighbor who owns a Yellow Labador. The RACHAEL is actually the patron saint, La Negrita sent to earth by God to care for Faust.

FAUST'S BROTHER:   Anti-war hippie who hates the upper white class.

FAUST'S MOTHER:   A simple woman who was born in Costa Rica.

FAUST'S FATHER:   A simple man who was born in Costa Rica.

YOUNG FAUST'S CLOSEST FRIEND:   Anti-war protestor.

BROWNIE:   Faust's dog.

OLD REGIS:   Rachael's dog with whom Faust forms a bond.

MICHAEL:   A soldier under Faust's command. A bitter dispute arises between the two when Faust lends him ten dollars which is not immediately

                                  paid back. For Michael's failure
                                  to repay the loan, Faust severely
                                  beats him up, putting him in the
                                  hospital for three days. After
                                  Michael's military discharge he
                                  becomes a drug addict, blaming
                                  Faust for his situation.

MEPHISTOPHELES:                   Satan who has taken pos-
                                  session of Faust's soul.


## Other Supporting Cast Members

6 to 8 American soldiers who reenact, through dance, the Battle of
An Loc that occurred during the Vietnam Easter Offensive of 1972.

6 to 8 North Vietnamese Army Regulars (NVA) who reenact, through
dance, the Battle of An Loc that occurred during the Vietnam Eastern
Offensive 1972.

                    (These same actors can dual play
                    the airport war protest scene.)



## SETTING

American Suburbia. An Loc, Vietnam.


## TIME FRAME

Present with backflashes to the Vietnam Eastern Offensive of 1972.

# CONTENTS

This play takes place during the Vietnam Easter Offensive of 1972, also known as the 1972 Spring-Summer Offensive. Some writers refer to the war as the Red Fiery summer. The Easter Offensive of 1972 lasted from March 30, 1972 through October 22, 1972. Faust, in this play, was involved in the Battle of An Loc, his time reference being from April 27th through May 17, 1972. The actual battle began on April 13, 1972 and ended on July 20, 1972. From May 17 until July 3, Faust and his men fought in Pleiku and Kontum, conducting three classified missions against the NVA's 320 Division as support troops to the ARVN's 22 Division, coordinated by the Korean White Horse Division. In early June the special ops team shifted their operations to Quang Tri where the fighting ended up in a stalemate. To this day the operation remains top secret. To understand the Eastern Offensive better, please read Walter Schenck's "extraordinarily brilliant existential novel", (Kirkus Book Reviews) *The Birdcatcher.*

The play, "Faust" borrowers the names from Goethe's play. The hook is redemption and like Goethe's Faust, the Main Character needs the help of divine intervention, provided through the loving attention of Costa Rica's patron saint, La Negrita. As the author is both Costa Rican and German it felt right to utilize his heritage in this manner.

During the late '60's and early '70's, violent war protesting and peaceful marching against the Vietnam War and racial turmoil took place on a nearly daily basis. During that era of strife, racial inequality, racial tensions, and the Civil Rights Movement, clashes between the police and the war protestors dominated American society. To stand up for freedom is the greatest reason for mankind's forward achievement.

Therefore, considering the time period and historic events of that era, it is impossible to render this play as politically correct. Offensive language consisting of harsh cuss words and bigotry was a common pattern during that time. The sad thing is, bigotry still exists even after such great sacrifices of life in war-torn countries thousands of miles away from the United States. Today, as then, intense and overt physical movements continue to occur between the patriotic conservative movement and the liberal marchers.

From 1967 and throughout the 1970's, Vietnam Veterans were unappreciated and scorned. This disregard, abrasive attitude, and abusive practices against the Vietnam Veterans lasted until the Kuwait War.

Capturing the intensity of those times requires a thorough unpeeling of the emotional duress of the actors portraying the characters. The emotional experience may be too much for some people, but to capture the heart and essence of that time-period, such unveilings are demanded.

Today, Vietnam is a thriving trading partner of the United States. If only the two Korea's can gain such a historic unification. If only the world can somehow gain long-sought peace. If only.

Special consideration must also be given to my readings of many other plays, drawing inspiration from them. Johann Wolfgang Von Goethe's The Tragedy of Heinrich Faust: Parts 1 & 2. A Christmas Carol by Charles Dickens. The movie, All Dogs Go TO Heaven, and of course, my own award-winning short story, Old Regis.

ACT 1

Scene 1

SETTING:                        Inside a darkened room a single
                                plastic chair rests near the
                                entry door.

AT RISE:                        Blue stage light shines on
                                FAUST, a Hispanic male, and
                                MARGARET, lovingly dancing in
                                each other's arms. She is
                                laughing happily as they twirl
                                in delight.


                        MARGARET
I still get the shivers being in your arms, handsome, old
man.


                        FAUST
You say that to all Hispanics, baby, because you know we're
the only real men on the face of the earth.

                (MARGARET laughs as she twirls out
                of his arms.)

                        MARGARET
I have to cook dinner. Won't take me long. Besides, aren't
you more German than Hispanic?

                (FAUST nods as he continues to mock
                dance by himself. Unexpected
                knocking occurs on the door.)

                        FAUST
What? Neighbors complaining because we're making too much
noise?

                        MARGARET
                (Offstage.)
Well, find out. Open the door.

                (FAUST opens the door.)

                    TELEGRAPH MAN
                     (Offstage.)
Mr. Faust?


                         FAUST
Of course. Who else?


                    TELEGRAPH MAN
                     (Offstage.)
Telegram. It's marked urgent. Please sign.


                         FAUST
Telegram? Who gets a telegram in today's world. Who sent
it?


                    TELEGRAPH MAN
                     (Offstage.)
A Mr. Mephistopheles. Sign here.


                         FAUST
     (Walks to center of stage as he rips open the telegram.
      Becomes deadly silent as he stares at the audience.)

                    (Reads out loud directly
                       to the audience.)
                    *Sergeant Alan Wagner died this morning*
                    *from Non-Hodgkin's Lymphoma as a result*
                    *of exposure to Agent Orange in the*
                    *providence of An Loc, Vietnam, 1972.*

                    (FAUST crumples up the telegram and
                    throws it hard onto the stage floor.
                    His left hand begins trembling. He
                    touches his chin, cheeks, nose,
                    face.)

                         FAUST
Now it's my turn. What I pledged in blood in Vietnam
remains valid.

                    (Intense activity occurs behind him
                    as cast members run about the stage
                    carrying ficus trees, bamboo trees,
                    banana trees, and other thick-green
                    plants. War sounds intensify as the
                    stage lights grow dim. FAUST begins
                    crying. He bolts from the center of

(the stage to the rear of the stage, mingling with the plants.)

                    FAUST
Find me, demon of demons!

                 MEPHISTOPHELES
                 (Off Stage.)
Find you? I have never lost track of you.

        (Afraid, FAUST leaps out from the
        plants. He stumbles and ends up on
        his knees. He then slams his fist
        into his palm several times.)

                    FAUST
FUCK YOU! GODDAMN YOU! I'll not come easy.

                 MEPHISTOPHELES
                 (Off Stage.)
You already have. Aren't you, at this very moment, dying?

        (Loud gun-battle sounds erupt off
        stage along with Cobra air strikes.
        Offstage, SOLDIERS can be heard
        screaming.

        A cacophony of variant-color lights
        hit the stage, focusing on the
        single plastic chair near the entry
        door of the stage.

        FAUST shakes intensely as his eyes
        peer at the audience. He begins to
        walk to the chair near the entry
        door. He picks up the chair and on
        his way back to the center of the
        stage he picks up the crumpled
        telegram. He places the chair down,
        sits in it, and smooths the
        telegram. He stares vacantly into
        the corner of the stage.)

                    FAUST
So you've got Wagner's soul.
        (FAUST stands up from the chair and
        steps a few feet away.)

Mephistopheles. I heard you have sensitive ears, all that terrible silence in Tartarus. Here's my gift to you.)
                    (FAUST stomps his feet as hard as he
                    can on the stage floor in a dance-
                    like fashion.)
Come on, MOTHERFUCKER! Come, MOTHEFUCKER!
                    (Pauses as he softens his voice.)
Mother . . . fuck . . . er. Where are you. Your ears okay?
                    (FAUST calms down as he stares again
                    at the audience.)
For you, alone, Mephistopheles, permit me to perform The Dance of Death. This dance I dance as an imploration for remembrance!
                    (FAUST dances intensely, clapping
                    his hands as his feet vigorously
                    stomp the floor. Suddenly he
                    pauses.)
Now, hear my desires! God, I desire. I turn now to GOD. Listen as I dance a dance for God's remembrance of who I am. I dance for redemption!

                                        (Enter       MEPHISTO-
                                        PHELES    holding    a
                                        legal document.)


                         MEPHISTOPHELES
I knew you would try to break your contract. Many do, when I come. All have failed.


                             FAUST
I survived every battle. I even survived the volcanoes' wrath.


                         MEPHISTOPHELES
It is I who placed the umbrella of protection over you.


                             FAUST
*Did you?* Or, took advantage of my fears. Who, suffering terror, does not call out to be saved by any force powerful enough to save?

REDEMPTION! Mephistopheles!

                         MEPHISTOPHELES
Never for you.

                              FAUST
Forsake your vow of keeping me alive! Longevity is a curse.
I survived, and how I dread having survived! Let go of my
soul!

                                        (Enter          MASKED
                                        SOLDIERS   OF   DEATH.
                                        They   gather   behind
                                        him,  joining  him  in
                                        his dance.)

                    (The MASKED SOLDIERS OF DEATH form a
                    diagonal "V" behind FAUST and in a
                    coordinated, dynamic range of foot
                    stomping, clapping, and the lifting
                    of arms.)

               FIRST MASKED SOLDIER OF DEATH
RAGE! Take it away!

               SECOND MASKED SOLDIER OF DEATH
HATE! Take it away!

               THIRD MASKED SOLDIER OF DEATH
BETRAYAL. Take it away!

               FOURTH MASKED SOLDIER OF DEATH
AGONY. Take it away!

                          TOGETHER
          (Their foot stomping and clapping cease
            as they form a circle around MEPHISTOPHELES.)
Redemption, Redemption, Redemption.

                       MEPHISTOPHELES
Not for any of you! Faust, you signed a contract . . . your
blood your eternal ink.
                            FAUST
          (Spreads his arms over his head.)
SALVATION! Gabriel, protect me. Look around me. My world is
filled with protecting ghosts. Raphael, send this hideous
monstrosity back to Tartarus! *Ci-Devant.*

                                        (The MASKED SOLDIERS
                                        OF   DEATH   rapidly
                                        exit,  removing  the
                                        plants with them.)

>               (FAUST walks back to the chair, picks
>               it up, and slams it on the floor. He
>               doubles down crying. He stretches
>               himself prostrate on the floor. The
>               stage darkens. FAUST stops crying as
>               he remains prostrate on the floor.)

                         FAUST [CON'T]
MARGARET! Where are you. God, I need you. MARGARET!

>                                   (Exit
>                                   MEPHISTOPHELES.)
>
>                                   (Enter MARGARET. She
>                                   sees the telegram in
>                                   his hand. She takes
>                                   it  from  him  and
>                                   reads it.)

                         MARGARET
                (She lies down next to him.)
You knew Wagner was dying.

                         FAUST
I knew. But then, I didn't know.

                         MARGARET
It's best he died. His suffering is over.

                         FAUST
But what about my suffering? My anguish? That shit-ass
Agent Orange drenched me at the same time it did Wagner.

                         MARGARET
The VA's trying to help you.

                         FAUST
Margaret, I'm dying from a chronic, incurable, blood
cancer. It's affecting my organs. My brain. I see things,
hear things too frightening to imagine. This world is too
delusional for me to live in.

                         MARGARET
I've never seen you so afraid. You've seen many men die,
yet, now that it's your turn, you're scared. Why?

                    FAUST
My cursed soul belongs to the demon! Long after my consumed
heart disappears into the voids of nothingness, my soul
will remain trapped in a vicious cycle of hideous torment.

                  MARGARET
Don't say such things.

                    FAUST
It's your fault I lost my soul.

                  MARGARET
We all lose our hearts to those we love.

                    FAUST
No. I mean it literally. For you, for a long life, I made a
bargain with the devil, the pledge signed in blood. Now,
there is no salvation, no redemption for my selfish
contract.

                  MARGARET
Honey. You signed a contract with a special attorney to
help you with you lawsuit against VA for having been denied
your Agent Orange claim. VA blames your disease on family
inheritance and the comingling of the ash of the volcanic
eruption of Irazu in '63 in Costa Rica. Faust, your
attorney asked you to sign a contract so he can coordinate
and access the reports of what the doctors are doing to
treat you for the Chagas parasites that invaded your body
underneath the trees that protected you from Irazu's fiery
lava which destroyed your village, Tarus.

                    FAUST
No, the attorney is a hideous thing in disguise. He's
Mephistopheles, the demon.

                  MARGARET
Mr. Mephistopheles is our attorney. He works on our behalf.
The last two decades VA has blamed everything that is wrong
with you on the parasites in Costa Rica. They refute your
Agent Orange bathing in Vietnam as they have no record of
it.

                    FAUST
How can they have a record when my missions were classified?

MARGARET

I'm here to do whatever I can for you. Just stop pushing me away when I try to help you. Please, share these remaining years with me, loving me. Respecting me. Let us both live as best as we can while we can.


FAUST

Live? How can I live when I'm dying? Of all the men who fought alongside me in An Loc, Kontum, and in Pleiku, I'm the only one still alive. Me. The stupid one. The foreigner . . . El *teniente primero* . . . who couldn't speak English well enough to command his own unit. I fucked up so badly. . . . I fucked them all up.
>(FAUST stands up.)

*I-ê! I-ê!*
>(FAUST begins stomping his feet as he performs a timed cadence military honor guard routine. FAUST sharply salutes on each pivotal military movement. He first executes a pivotal turn facing the left, shouting:)

*A la izquierda.*
>(He then pivots to the right, shouting:)

*A la derecho.*
>(He faces the audience as he follows up with another shout:)

*Al frente!*
>(FAUST pauses, turns his head, then softly whispers.)

*Pedazos de hijos de puta.*


MARGARET

Honey, I don't speak Spanish.


FAUST

You've been married to me for nearly thirty years, and still you don't speak Spanish?


MARGARET

It's America. U.S.A. . . . Not Costa Rica. Not Nicaragua. And, certainly, not Mexico. . . . U.S.A.


(FAUST laughs.)

                              FAUST
The country I fought for. The country my men died for. The
country I'm dying for.
                    (To Himself.)
Mephistopheles got me cheap.


                            MARGARET
                    (Misunderstanding.)
You think you got me cheap? I always thought of myself as
high maintenance. A beautiful woman needs beautiful things.


                              FAUST
You are beautiful. For you I've given my soul. For life to
live beside you, I've given my soul. Still, for having
surrendered my soul, how is it I'm dying? The body and the
soul are two, not one, yet I never felt if there were two
parts of me. Margaret, will you give up your life for me as
Alcestis offered to give up her life for Admetus?


                            MARGARET
My body, yes. My soul, never.


                              FAUST
Don't I deserve from you everything you have to give me?


                            MARGARET
I love you with all my heart.


                              FAUST
But not your soul?


                            MARGARET
Honey, all of me belongs to you. All of me. All that I am,
is yours. When will you accept that?


                              FAUST
Will you put it in writing with your own blood as I did?


                            MARGARET
That's going too far. When did you ever bleed for me?


                              FAUST
My overgrown spleen bleeds for you. My failing liver I give
to you before it totally fails. My mushy brain, I give it
without hesitation. But my intellect, my gall bladder, my
legs, my arms, my fingers, my hands, those parts of me, I
want.

                    (Pauses as he looks at MARGARET.)
Can't cut the grass overwise.


                         MARGARET
Or . . . hug me . . . when I need to be hugged. Kiss me. I
need to be kissed.
                    (FAUST affectionately kisses her.
                    Suddenly,  MARGARET  breaks  down
                    crying as she hugs him tightly. She
                    pushes him back as she breaks away
                    to run to the right front of the
                    stage. She raises her hands to the
                    ceiling, pleading frenetically.)
Oh, God. Oh, God. Help him. Help him.


                    (She walks toward the back of the
                    stage, sobbing.)


                              (Enter
                              MEPHISTOPHELES.)


                         MEPHISTOPHELES
As I had promised, she loves you with all her essence. As I
had promised you, the most beautiful woman that you wanted in
your life, is in your life. And now, you cry because your
well-lived life is coming to an end.


                         FAUST
Wagner and I should have both died in An Loc. A lot of misery
would have been averted had I perished fifty years ago.


                         MEPHISTOPHELES
Then you should never have called for me. Never begged for
an extension of life. Never begged for Margaret. Never
begged for a prominent position at the bank. Never begged
me for as many things as you begged me for. Whatever you
wanted I gave without hesitation.


                         FAUST
Why? There's nothing special about my soul. It's like all the
other souls. A flash of light. A sparkle of intuition. A
breath of radiance which I had never seen emitted, even though
I had seen many deaths. There is nothing unique or wondrous
about my soul.

MEPHISTOPHELES
Except that God also wants it. But you pledged your contract to me, not to God. I own you because you asked me to own you.

FAUST
Then heal me fully. I don't want this agony to continue. My entire body aches with ravaging pain. You want me, heal me.

MEPHISTOPHELES
I cannot heal you. Only God can heal you. But you turned away from him to fulfill all your earthly desires. Therefore, die with your decision.

FAUST
Die I shall, but not according to your desires. You shall not have my soul. I give it to God.

MEPHISTOPHELES
God? He doesn't want it anymore. You're a man covered in the pleasures of sin. Wait. Let me prove it. Let me be the first to call God to you. If he comes and you actually reconcile yourself to him, I'll tear up the contract. But believe me, he'll never come for you.

   (Stage projector suddenly shines on
   the wall a picture of La Negrita,
   the Patron Saint of Costa Rica.)

MEPHISTOPHELES
(Screaming.)
What is this damnable interference! The bargain has already been struck.

LA NEGRITA
Faust, all you have to do is ask for my help. Nothing more.

FAUST
(Gasping in surprise,
he folds his arms over his chest
as he bows his head.)
La Negrita . . . Black Madonna . . . La Virgen de los Angeles de Costa Rica . . . help me.

(LIGHTS FADE.)

(CURTAINS.)

(END OF ACT 1.)

ACT 2

Scene 1

SETTING:                        Outside FAUST'S house.

AT RISE:                        Enter FAUST pacing back and
                                forth.


                         FAUST
                (Talks through the door.)
I'm bored. I'm bored. I need to do something.

                         MARGARET
                       (O.S.)
Wanna go for a drive?

                         FAUST
Too many young crazies on the road. They think 45 miles an
hour means 65 miles an hour: twist-and-shout, turn-and-slam
those brakes. And, when they see this old, fat, bald, ugly
Hispanic, they think it's killing time.

                         MARGARET
                  (O.S. Laughing.)
Well, wasn't it you who once told me you were the target of
many enemies. You can't still be afraid of dying after all
the things you went through—and miraculously survived. God
must really love you.

                         FAUST
Baby, it's the demons who love me. I'm their favorite
person.

                                        (MARGARET enters the
                                        room, buttoning her
                                        blouse.)


                         MARGARET
Stop exaggerating. It's me they want. Not you.
                  (Pauses. Smiles.)
You, they may have, but me, they don't have.

                         FAUST
Come on, baby, put up your fists.
                    (Mock boxing.)
Wait up. Hold on, baby . . . you win. You win.
                    (Both tenderly kiss. FAUST faces the
                    audience with a wry smile.)
This is why I married a pure, beautiful, woman! If anyone
can save me from my curse, it's you.


                         MARGARET
                    (Smiles.)
I have no power to save anyone. If you're now looking for
some sort of reconciliation with your past, I can't offer
it to you. Oh, I can caress you, listen to your troubles,
hold your hand, share your tears, but I can't purge from
you the things upsetting you.


                         FAUST
                    (Smiles.)
Margaret, peace for a piece?


                         MARGARET
No time for a piece so you can have peace because I have to
sweep.


                                        (MARGARET  exits  and
                                        immediately   returns
                                        with a broom.)


                         FAUST
Sweeping up the sidewalk . . . or getting ready to hit me?


                         MARGARET
Why would I ever want to hit you? Just because you're on a
guilt trip for being alive? I wanted a handsome man, and a
handsome man I got. Now, I have to sweep the sidewalk on
account of our neighbor blowing all his leaves onto our
side of the street.


                         FAUST
                    (Reflectively.)
Margaret, did we make a mistake marrying each other? I
mean, you had to take on yourself so many of my problems
which you never knew I had, while I had no burdens to take
on when I married you. I was already starting to lose my
hair, while yours kept on getting fuller and more radiant.

I think I married perfection while you married
imperfection.

                        MARGARET
Maybe we did make a mistake marrying each other. You never
tell me what to do, yet you always manage to do everything
I ask of you. Yes, we're definitely unbalanced. I think we
should argue about things and stop agreeing with each other
on everything. We should be throwing rocks at each other.
Burn the dinner. Bleach the color clothes. Never iron. Live
a pig style. Yes, that's what we'll do.

                        FAUST
Maybe we should go to bed and discuss it some more.

                        MARGARET
I agree. Now, corrupt me to no end.

                        FAUST
How in the world can you possibly love a fat, ugly, bald
old man who's the incarnation of everything wrong in the
world?

                        MARGARET
I don't know. Maybe the devil put a spell on me.

                        FAUST
Yes, he did.

                        MARGARET
                      (Smiles.)
Then in that case I better go outside to sweep up the
leaves laying in the gutter before you try to cast any more
spells over me.

                        FAUST
You know, I really hate myself for having enslaved you to
me, against your will, yet that's how badly I wanted you in
my life.

                        MARGARET
Do you love me enough to get rid of your Spanish accent?

                  (They affectionately hug again as
                  they share another kiss.)

FAUST
Hey, you ever stop to think how long it took me to learn
how to articulate "thought" from "fought", "bee" from
"free", "dice" from "nice", never mind how to pronounce
"refrigerator" a la "alligator".

MARGARET
I'm not impressed, college-graduate, and an officer and a
gentleman, Captain, sir. When you can pronounce
"arrederci," then, I'll be impressed.

FAUST
(Fast.)
Try this one out: "I thought I fought the good fight to be
free before a bee could sting me." Hmmmmm?

MARGARET
No. You try this one out: If you get in my face when I'm in
the mood to sweep, I'll beat you in your nose and whump you
to kingdom come.

FAUST
You got me beat, whumping girl . . . pitter-patter of my
heart. Mmmmm.

MARGARET
My, my. You really are bored. By the way, doesn't someone
in the neighborhood owe you a thousand dollars for having
fixed up his car? Overdue, right?

FAUST
(Reflective.)
For Michael's sake, Thomas owes me nothing.

MARGARET
Michael? Who is Michael?

FAUST
Strange, isn't it. Michael? I don't know why I brought up
his name.

MARGARET
Well? Who is he?

                    FAUST
He was someone who once borrowed ten dollars from me,
refused to pay me back, and suffered the consequences of
his refusal.

                  MARGARET
Oh? And?

                    FAUST
And, nothing. He gravely offended me in front of my men,
weakening my position as their commander, so I corrected
things.

                  MARGARET
What did you do?

                    FAUST
What I always do when confronted.

                  MARGARET
Oh. You beat him up, didn't you? Badly?

                    FAUST
Yes. Badly. Thank God Wagner was there. Now, let the issue
rest.

                  MARGARET
Are you getting angry with me?

                    FAUST
No. It just I'm suddenly occupied with all these unwanted
memories. They flash in front of me when I don't want them,
and just linger in my mind long after I want them gone.

                  MARGARET
Then you really do need to make new friends. Go on, then.
Explore the neighborhood. Talk to new people. Mingle. If
you're really bored, drive to church, find God, confess.

                    FAUST
Make friends with the neighbors? They're going to think I'm
either trying to sell them cocaine or wanting to cut their
grass. As for church, the priest will have a heart attack
seeing me sitting in the pew. Or, the church building may
just fall down on top of me.

MARGARET
(Concerned.)
Don't cut anyone's grass. Your body's too weak.

FAUST
I'll stay home and help you sweep up the leaves.

MARGARET
No. Go and meet the neighbors. Just don't get seduced –
handsome.
FAUST
If tempted, I won't resist.

MARGARET
You better resist. The broom handle is strong.

FAUST
Lord, lead me forth as I walk through the valley of death.
Just don't allow me to meet Mephistopheles on the way to
heaven, because that devil never gives back change.

(Exit.)

(LIGHTS FADE.)

(CURTAINS.)

(END OF SCENE 1.)

ACT 2

Scene 2

SETTING:                          Outside in the neighborhood.

AT RISE:                          Enter FAUST, wiping his face.


                    FAUST
                (To the audience.)
Man, I don't know why I picked such a hot day to walk.
                (Pauses.)
Man, I never knew this neighborhood was so big. I must have
passed a thousand houses, and not one person, anywhere is
outside.
                (Pauses.)
I'm an idiot. A dying, old, fat, idiot. Or maybe these
*hombres y jefes*, when they see this dark-skinned foreigner
walking around, hide themselves behind their doors?

If that's the case, they're faster than Jessie Owens or
Usain Bolt. Maybe they're diving into their swimming pools
like Joaquin Capilla himself?

*Estupidos*!

Man. Why didn't I build a pool? A koi pond too, surrounded
by a large flagstone patio with an outdoor kitchen.
                (Pauses.)
No. All I got is a rotting old-wooden swing and a rusty
barbecue grill not used three times in fifteen years.
                (Pauses.)
Yeah, Wagner. You were right to die when you did.
                (Pauses.)
Before I take another step forward, I'm going back home for
a frozen bottle of water.

                                (Exit.)

                                (LIGHTS FADE.)

                                (CURTAINS.)

                                (END OF SCENE 2.)

ACT 2

Scene 3

SETTING:                          The front of RACHEL'S house
                                  with a yellow Labrador tied
                                  outside.

AT RISE:                          Enter FAUST, still wiping his
                                  face, carrying a bottle of
                                  frozen water.

                                  He cautiously walks up to the
                                  old dog, extending his
                                  handkerchief for the dog to
                                  smell.


                            FAUST
Hey, boy. Hey. It's okay. Yeah, it's okay.
          (FAUST pets hard the dog's sides and
          vigorously shakes his head.)
There, there, boy. All you need is a little attention.

                                  (Enter RACHAEL. She
                                  is wearing an old
                                  sweater and worn
                                  shoes.)

                            RACHAEL
I don't know why that dog doesn't bite you, a stranger and
all.

                            FAUST
Dogs like me.

                            RACHAEL
Do they? I think it's that bottle of half frozen water in
your hand that he likes. Pour a little on the ground for
him to drink.
          (FAUST obeys her, then takes a sip
          for himself.)
Here. My bottle of water's hot. Give me yours.
          (FAUST again obeys her. She opens
          the cap and take a sip.)
Refreshing.
          (FAUST drinks from the hot bottle.)

Warm water doesn't bother you?

                    FAUST
No. I drank a lot of warm water.

                    RACHAEL
I'm walking to the grocery store. Before you came up to the
dog, I realized I left my purse in the house. I need ten
dollars.

                    FAUST
              (Pulls out his wallet.)
What is it with ten dollars. Not twenty, not twenty-five,
not one, or five. Always ten dollars. Here.

                    RACHAEL
I'll pay you back.

                    FAUST
No. It's a gift. Buy doggie a treat.

          (FAUST returns to petting the dog.)

                    RACHAEL
              (Looking at her dog.)
You know, don't you, it ain't too smart for you to keep on
shaking him up like that.

                    FAUST
He loves the attention.

                    RACHAEL
He ain't got much longer on this earth.

                    FAUST
Neither do I.

                    RACHAEL
Oh? Well, then best move on. I don't want Regis eating up
your corpse.

                    FAUST
Regis? Old Regis.

                    RACHAEL
Regis. Nothing more.

                    FAUST
I like dogs. The dog seems to like you. So, you're okay. No
problems.

                                        (Exit.)

                                        (LIGHTS FADE.)

                                        (CURTAINS.)

                                        (END OF SCENE 3.)

ACT 2

Scene 4

SETTING:                    In front of RACHAEL'S house.
                            REGIS tied outside.

AT RISE:                    Enter   FAUST   carrying   a
                            pocketful of dog biscuits. He
                            places a few at REGIS' feet.


                    FAUST
Hey, good? *Si, es verdad. Muy Bueno.*


                            (Enter RACHAEL.)

                    RACHAEL
I see you found my house. Tracking me for your money?

                    FAUST
No. I just happened by, hoping to find Old Regis again.

                    RACHAEL
You're ruining his appetite.

                    FAUST
It's just a few. No *mass* . . . I mean . . . not more than
these.

            (RACHAEL walks up to him.)

                    RACHAEL
Don't be making a nuisance out of yourself. Regis isn't
going to be of any use to me if he allows strangers to walk
right up to my property.

                    FAUST
I understand. You have a beautiful yard. Big, red roses,
camellias, Pink Myrtles. A Chinese Rainbow Tree.
Impressive. I love your yard.

                    RACHAEL
You garden?

                         FAUST
I plant. I reflect. I visualize. Gardening helps me to cope
when I remember things that I never want to remember.


               (Begins to choke up with emotion.)

                        RACHAEL
                   (Interpreting.)
. . . Bad things?

               (FAUST nods, nearly teary eyed.)

                         FAUST
Yeah. Bad things.
                   (Turns away.)
Your garden seems as if it came from heaven itself. I have
never seen such a beautiful, harmonic yard. A perfectly
balanced yard.


                        RACHAEL
Don't flatter me. I don't need it.


                         FAUST
I apologize. I was trying to be friendly. You know, it's
not easy for me to be friendly with other people . But I'm
trying.


                        RACHAEL
Is it people you want to associate with, or my Regis?


                         FAUST
Regis holds a strange bond over me. It's been years since I
bothered to pet a dog.


                        RACHAEL
You should get your own and leave mine alone.


                              (Exit   RACHAEL.   As
                              she  opens  her  door
                              wide,  and  a  statue
                              of   Costa   Rica's
                              patron   saint,   La
                              Negrita, is seen.)


                         FAUST
Wait. How is it you have a statue of La Negrita? Are you
Costa Rican?

                         RACHAEL
Been there. Been many places.


                          FAUST
Me too.


                         RACHAEL
I know. I went to your house. It's big. Curious, I learned
where you used to work. Your wife's job. Everything.


                          FAUST
Yeah. And probably before the hour was up after you found
my house.


                         RACHAEL
Actually, within thirty minutes. You're something else.
Silver Star, Bronze Star. Army Commendation Medal. Two
tours in 'Nam. A Captain before you left Special Forces.
Not too many Hispanics can say that.


                          FAUST
And not one Costa Rican. How did you end up being so nosey?


                         RACHAEL
Your wife asked my friend to look after you.


                          FAUST
My wife never mentioned you.


                         RACHAEL
That's because she never met me. My friend tells me you
have a violent temper. Breaking chairs. Cursing. Throwing
rocks into the lake. Walking around during the night all by
yourself, muttering weird stuff.


                          FAUST
It's like that. Yes. But I never hurt anyone. Just myself.


                         RACHAEL
And despite being an anti-social fiend, my old mutt becomes
your friend. Interesting. See you tomorrow.

(Exit.)

(LIGHTS FADE.)

(CURTAINS.)

(END OF SCENE 4.)

ACT 2

Scene 5

SETTING:                          Inside FAUST'S living room, a
                                  wall is covered with pictures
                                  of Paris, London, Rome.

AT RISE:                          Enter FAUST. He heads directly
                                  to a small table to examine a
                                  few porcelain dogs plus a small
                                  statue of Costa  Rica's patron
                                  saint, *La Negrita*. He picks it
                                  up and speaks directly to it.


                              FAUST
Tell me, Rachael: How is it you came to have such a dog as
Regis? How? If only you can see that I also have my own
Regis.
                    (FAUST holds the porcelain high.)
Rachael, my Aunt Catharine, bought for me my own Regis on
my seventh birthday. A glorious animal. A masterful dog.
One filled with affection for me, in spite of how horrid I
had become. Like a magical script from a heart revealed, I
kept that dog for sixteen years. It followed me everywhere,
never tethered, never scolded, never shouted at. He knew
exactly how to act. How to come home. How to meet me after
school hours. In my class, Rachael, only I owned such a
treasure. A story book realized.
                    (FAUST  places  the  porcelain  dog
                     gently on the table.)
And here, Rachael, even in this neighborhood of such
elegant houses, lives striving and thriving, there is the
presence of evil lurking about. I'm the only Hispanic in
this neighborhood. Oh, there are a few Asians, but the
neighbor's prejudice toward me glows like a torch. Hatred
is inextinguishable no matter where I live.

Rachael, that statue of Costa Rica's patron Saint, La
Negrita, how do you happen to have it? Coincidence? If only
you knew my mother's prayer to her on my behalf. But then,
perhaps you do? No. Impossible. What does it matter. Life
extinguishes, but never the soul. You have Regis. I have
Margaret. But for how long will we have them. Or, for that
matter, how long will Regis have you and how long will
Margaret have me?

How is it that I became such a miserable and selfish person to everyone I love? I can't remember the last time I shared a heart-felt conversation with Margaret.

>                 (FAUST sits down, rests his head on
>                 the small table. Falls asleep.)

>                             (LIGHTS FADE.)

>                             (CURTAINS.)

>                             (END OF ACT 2.)

ACT 3

Scene 1

SETTING:                          Inside FAUST'S living room.

AT RISE:                          Enter a ghost, WAGNER.


                    WAGNER
Wake up, my still living friend.

                    FAUST
                  (Groaning.)
Wagner? I thought you were dead.

                    WAGNER
I am. And soon, yourself also.

                    FAUST
As if I need reminding. So, tell me, old friend, did you
come to assure me I'll be in heaven? Even one such as I?
Or, destined to hell where I belong, fried to a crisp for
pigs to feast on?

                    WAGNER
The pigs will vomit consuming you. You're too mean-spirited
for heaven, yet, too gentle for hell. However, your love
for that dog—Regis—gives you hope for redemption. Through
redemption, comes salvation.

                    FAUST
Wagner, don't lecture me on redemption, nor on salvation.
I've killed too many men. Sinned far too many times to
believe in such stupidities. If God is all-loving, then why
am I still here? God should have long ago killed me,
thereby, saving the lives of so many others more deserving
of life than I.

                    WAGNER
A man who survived everything complains about surviving
everything.

                    FAUST
As you did. Until . . . well, until.

                         WAGNER
I'm curious. Why do you love that dog as much as you do?

                         FAUST
I have no love for that old thing. I just feel sorry for
it. Dogs need real friends.

                         WAGNER
Truly?

                         FAUST
Yes. Dogs can sense friends from enemies.

                         WAGNER
Meaning, you're remembering how to show affection, stepping
away from your indifference toward others.

                         FAUST
Meaning nothing.
                    (Pauses.)
Wagner, why are you in my dreams?

                         WAGNER
To remind you of things best not forgotten.

                         FAUST
                   (Laughing.)
Why do you want to do that? Because I pet an old dog?

                         WAGNER
You've shown that your heart still cares, and caring, you
can still be saved from being eternally damned to Gehenna.

                         FAUST
Do you think I should be saved from hell when hell is
exactly where I belong?

                         WAGNER
From the remotest, dismal embers of a forest fire, still
life emerges. In the hottest deserts, in the coldest
regions of earth, inside the deepest oceans, life thrives.

                         FAUST
Life thrives? You're dead. Now, please leave my rotting
soul alone. Mephistopheles is calling for it. Find your
peace and leave me to my bitterness.

                         WAGNER
Margaret, your wife, petitioned God to save you from
yourself.


                         FAUST
When? Margaret never prays. At least, not as far as I'm
aware.


                         WAGNER
On the morning that you received the telegram of my death.


                         FAUST
I remember.


                         WAGNER
I found it curious that in your room of solitude, you chose
Rachael to think about as you examined your porcelain
figurines.


                         FAUST
She is not normal, that woman. The dog shouldn't be in her
care.


                         WAGNER
You're right, on both counts. Rachel is not a normal woman,
and that dog does belong in your care. But you have to earn
it first. And to earn Regis, you have to appease Rachael.


                         FAUST
And just how do I do that?


                         WAGNER
By accompanying me this night. By sharing with me things of
the past that you refuse to share with anyone. By finding
within those sharing moments, rectification of your sins,
thereby leading you to reconciliation with God. With
yourself.


                         FAUST
Why?


                         WAGNER
Because Margaret made a sincere petition on your behalf,
and, through the power of love, God listened to her. He is
offering you a chance to set aside your contract with the
demon of demons. To do so, you need to reexperience your
life and undo the moments of terrible commitments.

                    FAUST
Upon a frightened wife's petition, you have the nerve to
ask for me to reveal to you a young man's heartbreaking
disclosure never shared with anyone before.


                    WAGNER
Yes. Also, because Rachael is eager to discover at what
point you contracted your soul to Mephistopheles.


                    FAUST
Come again? Rachael?


                    WAGNER
We know you signed the contract, but when? Before the bank
hired you? Before you got your job promotion? Before you
married Margaret? Before you went to Vietnam? While you
were in Vietnam? After Vietnam? In college?


                    FAUST
Easy. In Vietnam.


                    WAGNER
We need to know the precise moment. To do that, we have to
revisit the scene and there, undo your pledges to the
heartless demon. Only through this manner can we undo the
document which pledged your soul into the vices of the evil
one.


                    FAUST
I signed more than one. Several, actually. All are
unbreakable.


                    WAGNER
Nothing is unbreakable. Rachael will help you undo the
contracts . . . if you permit her.


                    FAUST
How?


                    WAGNER
By reversing time.

(LIGHTS FADE.)

(CURTAINS.)

(END OF SCENE 1.)

ACT 3

Scene 2

SETTING:                          Inside FAUST'S living room.

AT RISE:                          Enter YOUNG FAUST, dressed in
                                  military combat fatigues.


                    YOUNG FAUST
              (YOUNG FAUST speaks with
            a mystical tone of voice.)
In the age of draft-dodging to Canada, I volunteered to
serve in Vietnam to escape the dilemma and confusion of
American's hating Americans, only to be jettisoned to a
jungle of extreme prejudice, a nightmare's unfathomable
terror: the Battle of An Loc of '72.
                    (SOLDIERS from the right stage
                    dressed in camouflage with their
                    faces painted enter the stage behind
                    FAUST. From the left of the stage
                    VIETNAMESE SOLDIERS enter the stage
                    inside a dance sequence. Both groups
                    engage in fierce motions of
                    fighting, yet neither group speaks.
                    All the action proceeds silently as
                    if in a surreal world.)
From April-through-September a daily bombardment of flesh-
tearing hatred rained upon our units. Each day my unit, the
17th Combat Aviation Group, a unit of Cobras and Hueys,
failed to defeat General Giap's pincher assault. Our swift-
flying, sleek Cobras rendered the farmers' fields into a
plowed nightmare.
                    (The group of silent soldiers run
                    amok about the stage, their hands
                    stretching to the ceiling, toward
                    each other, toward the audience. All
                    the soldiers encircle FAUST, their
                    hands flaying about his body and
                    face. The group breaks off, suddenly
                    freezing in the various individual
                    random positions.)

                    YOUNG FAUST [CON'T]
Mortar rounds and precision bombings impacted all around
me.

                    (A soldier, YOUNG WAGNER, enters the
                    stage, handing YOUNG FAUST a heavy
                    machine gun. YOUNG FAUST drops to
                    the prone position as do the other
                    SOLDIERS.  The  NORTH  VIETNAMESE
                    ARMY—NVA—run to the aisles of the
                    theater.

                    (Rifles and mortar shells sounds are
                    exploding everywhere. Stage lights
                    go off-and-on chaotically.)

                    YOUNG FAUST {CON'T]
              (Screams to YOUNG WAGNER.)
My M-60's barrel is red-hot from its constant firing.

                        FIRST SOLDIER
          (Panic screaming as he runs across the stage.)
                    I don't wanna die.

                       SECOND SOLDIER
          (Runs across the stage from the other direction.)
                  Lieutenant! Help me. Help me!

                        THIRD SOLDIER
              (Joins the others onstage.
                    Simultaneously.)
              Come on, gook motherfuckers! Come on!

                        YOUNG WAGNER
Lieutenant. There're too many gooks! They're overtaking us!
Goddamn it, Faust. Look. Suicidal terrorists—Sappers— they
broke through our lines.

                    (The NVA whirl about the aisle.
                    Suddenly, all of them unleash a
                    coordinated fierce war shout which
                    turns into individual agonizing
                    shouts of pain.)

                        YOUNG FAUST
              (To the audience. Rapidly speaking.)
Our bloodied knives, our spent ammunition, our valiant
stance, useless. The attackers, dedicated to their Eastern

Offensive, hit their target: Pleiku's largest ammunition-storage facility. A deafening roar! A fling of mortars, ammunition, and bombs hurled hundreds of feet up, brilliantly brightening the darkness into a ghastly daylight. Tens-of-thousands armaments became a miniature duplication of Hiroshima.
>                     (Brutally loud explosions fill the
>                     stage. Bright red-and-yellow lights
>                     flicker. The NVA run about the front
>                     aisles then run to the back aisles
>                     while the AMERICAN SOLDIERS leap
>                     around YOUNG FAUST and YOUNG WAGNER,
>                     running and dancing about in
>                     fright.)

An Armageddon's consequence ensued throughout Vietnam as a result of Nixon's Vietnamization program, a presidential decision neither periled or heroic depending on Kissinger's judgment: true or false. The battle raged on. And on. Amputated bodies littered the roads, the hills, the makeshift graves impossible to forget. Miles of refugees, with nowhere to go, crowded the highways at Hue. Chaos a mere consequence of brutality.

                        FOURTH SOLDIER
Wagner. Behind you. Behind you.

>                     (An NVA rushes into the stage
>                     directly toward YOUNG WAGNER. They
>                     engage in a fight. YOUNG FAUST pulls
>                     the NVA off YOUNG WAGNER and strikes
>                     him dead with a knife.)

                        YOUNG WAGNER
Lieutenant! Please! There are too many of them. We can't hold them back.

                        SOLDIER
Lieutenant! I'm out of ammo.

                        YOUNG FAUST
Bayonets! Draw bayonets!
>                     (Fierce hand-to-hand fighting
>                     ensues in dance-like fashion,
>                     soldiers' bodies, writhing in
>                     agony, fall to the stage floor.)

Hold your positions! Hold! I don't give a damn if they kill
us ten times over! Hold your fucking positions!

>                    (A chaotic mingling of the NVA and
>                    SOLDIERS ensues, every soldier
>                    screaming death cries as they drop
>                    on the stage. "*I-ê! I-ê!*" Their
>                    torsos violently shiver as their
>                    legs kick about in wails of agony.)

YOUNG FAUST

Fuck! I don't wanna die. I'll do anything to live.
Devil may care, demon of hell, take my soul.
>                    (Cuts his wrist.)

This is my pledge to you.

>                              (Enter Rachael.)

RACHAEL

This is the first moment when you lost yourself to the
demonic powers. Take courage in yourself. Rewind and undo
what you did.

>                    (Stage goes pitch black. Super
>                    bright flashes cover the stage as if
>                    bomb bursts. The stage lights come
>                    on, barely shining. Among the
>                    numerous corpses YOUNG WAGNER and
>                    YOUNG FAUST remain unwounded. Blood
>                    covers their fatigues. Throughout
>                    the stage and aisles wounded men
>                    moan, one, covered in blood, is seen
>                    on the far left saying nothing but
>                    staring directly at the audience.
>                    Stage lights darken again, shining
>                    only on YOUNG FAUST, his uniform and
>                    face covered in globs of blood and
>                    soot.)

YOUNG FAUST
>                    (Looks at his arm.)

My wrist's wound has disappeared. I was afraid to die. I
shouldn't be alive, but I am alive. I am no longer afraid.

>                              (Exit Rachael.)

                         YOUNG FAUST [CON'T]
                        (To the audience.)
My service time in 'Nam finally concluded, the infamous
countdown, thirty days and a wake-up recited by all, the
last week's countdown, seven days and a wake-up being the
most treacherous.

                                        (Stage lights softly
                                        glow   as   all   the
                                        soldiers exit.)

                         YOUNG FAUST [CON'T]
    The first day I reached Fort Lewis, Washington, I settled
down in my quarters, received a physical, never mind the
stress . . . for who spoke of it then?
    The second day I went home, a five-hour flight through
cumulous-clouds thick with deceit.
    In my strapped chair, I shook violently, scared of
vomiting, scared of meeting a family I haven't seen or
talked to for over a year: so many personal views changed,
twisted, distorted. All I could think of was holding onto
some sort of former resemblance of a child they once knew.
    On the way back home, I kept struggling through the
eternal, mystical catch-of-time return-trip back home,
strapped to my seat inside an aluminum rocket with death-
defying wings.
    Trapped, my inner demons rendered that flight into an
intense fear that grabbed at my mind.
    To endure, to survive, I fantasized of landing to a
familiar home filled with grace and greenery, a
neighborhood solid, welcoming.
    Instead, when my friends at the airport saw my medals, my
uniform, they merely nodded.
                   (YOUNG FAUST begins crying.)
    Oh, God. Why am I so fucking useless?
So damn meaningless?

                                     (LIGHTS FADE.)

                                     (CURTAINS.)

                                     (END OF SCENE 2.)

ACT 3

Scene 3

SETTING:                          FAUST and WAGNER stand to the
                                  left side of the stage
                                  witnessing another reenactment
                                  of FAUST'S youth at the
                                  airport.

                                  There are four plastic chairs
                                  facing the audience and four
                                  behind those. Each chair is
                                  separated by a chair's width.
                                  The four people facing the
                                  audience are dressed in 60's
                                  clothing, holding closed
                                  umbrellas in their hands. The
                                  four people facing the rear
                                  wall are dressed in military
                                  clothing with rifles. Of
                                  course, the audience cannot
                                  see them, until the four
                                  exchange chairs.

AT RISE:                          Enter YOUNG FAUST and YOUNG
                                  FAUST'S CLOSEST FRIEND.


                    YOUNG FAUST'S CLOSEST FRIEND
Faust, you're an insult to your neighbors. You betrayed
your high-school class. I can't believe you volunteered to
be sent to 'Nam.

                            YOUNG FAUST
I respect and love my country.

                    YOUNG FAUST'S CLOSEST FRIEND
I never knew you were a fascist. A Hispanic fascist. Duty.
Honor. Country. Flag-waving and Pledge of Allegiance.

                            YOUNG FAUST
Man, we used to play basketball and soccer together. We're
a team.

                    YOUNG FAUST'S CLOSEST FRIEND
Not anymore. The army has you deep in its throat. And to
think, when you were the boxing champion at school, you
were the one who always won all your fights with your
powerful fists: crushed in your opponents' heads when you
thrust, jabbed, and slammed your uppercuts without let-up,
making me proud to be Hispanic. You really knew how to beat
up a guy, and for that, we all became your friends. So,
it's okay if you beat up some people in 'Nam, but did you
have to kill them, butchering them with a knife? Now,
you're the establishment's slave fighting in the
establishment's war.

                                        (Exit FAUST'S CLOS-
                                        EST FRIEND.

                    (The four people in the front chairs
                    exchange chairs with the military
                    dressed people.)

                                        (Enter FAUST'S BRO-
                                        THER.)

                         FAUST'S BROTHER
When are you getting rid of that filthy rag?

                           YOUNG FAUST
What rag?

                         FAUST'S BROTHER
Your military uniform. Costa Rican's never wear them.

                           YOUNG FAUST
I'm an American.

                         FAUST'S BROTHER
Don't say that too loud.

                                        (Enter         FAUST'S
                                        FATHER and MOTHER.)

                           YOUNG FAUST
Mom, does my uniform bother you?

                         FAUST'S MOTHER
It's an insult to peaceful humanity. Your brother's right.
As soon as we get home you need to change into some other

clothes. We're Hispanics and always will be no matter what we do. Look at your uncle. No one cares he served in Korea. No one cares your grandfather died in France during World War II, leaving behind a broken hearted, destitute wife. We're not respected. Understand me?

                    YOUNG FAUST
I need to stay in uniform. I'm still an officer in active service.


                    FAUST'S FATHER
For how long?


                    YOUNG FAUST
I have three years to go.


                    FAUST'S BROTHER
Have you ever thought of going back to Costa Rica? There are no extradition papers there. If you like wearing uniforms, you can become a cop there.


                    YOUNG FAUST
You just don't get it, do you.
                    (Pauses. To his MOTHER.)
Mom, I signed up for another tour to 'Nam.


                         (War    protestors    and    military
                         personnel exchange their positions
                         again.  They  begin  a  slow  counter
                         dance, depicting a fight.)


                    FAUST'S MOTHER
                    (Nearly shouting.)
What on heavens for? Haven't you done enough over there?


                    YOUNG FAUST
I left some friends behind.


                    FAUST'S MOTHER
Who cares about them. You have a family's responsibility here.


                    YOUNG FAUST
                    (To his FATHER.)
How's my dog, Brownie, doing?

FAUST'S FATHER
That dog's old. I don't know what keeps him alive.

YOUNG FAUST
(To his BROTHER.)
Wanna catch some balls when we get home?

FAUST'S BROTHER
No way, bro. I don't want my friends to see you. They think
you're still on base, or somewhere.

YOUNG FAUST
Why aren't you glad to see me. I'm your brother.

(The four people in the front chairs
again exchange chairs with the 60's-
dressed people. Their dance
movements are more pronounced.)

FAUST'S BROTHER
I read your letters. They're full of violence. You
shouldn't be using us to confess away your sins. You killed
too many people who were doing nothing more than trying to
protect their country from American manipulators.

YOUNG FAUST
What do you mean?

FAUST'S BROTHER
You're an officer. You should know better than all of us
that the people in power care nothing about anything except
how to make money while preserving their own stature. Man,
we're not invited to their parties, to their schools. We
can't even date rich girls. What are we? Light-skinned
niggers. They don't want us just as they don't want blacks,
or the Asians around them. The rich only want the gold
mines the Vietnamese have. That, and their rice fields.
Wake up to reality, bro.

(In the rear of the stage the light
shines on a PILOT, STEWARDESS, and
four to six BUSINESSMEN.

The actors, sitting in the two sets
of rows, suddenly stand up, lifting
their plastic chairs to above their
right shoulders, in a threatening

manner toward each other. The
SOLDIERS perform a military step
while the WAR PROTESTORS perform
loose steps until all 8 actors spin
their chairs around, slamming them
hard on the stage. A competitive
dance ensues, parting only when the
BUSINESSMEN, PILOT, and STEWARDESS
dance among them.)

                    FAUST
                (To himself.)
To be rich. Powerful. An important man. I'll give my soul
for that. Satan, make me wealthy. I'll be yours forever.

                        (Enter RACHAEL.)

                    RACHAEL
Rewind those words. Step back a second time and redirect
yourself.

                (All the ACTORS freeze as the lights
                dim. A bright red stage light up and
                focuses on FAUST, slowly turning
                green as he speaks.)

                    FAUST
                (To himself.)
To be rich. Powerful. An important man. Well, leave that to
those who want it. I'll just live out my life as best as I
can and place my trust in God.

                        (Exit RACHAEL.)

                        (MAIN ACTORS move to
                        left stage into the
                        dark.)


                (Enter A NEW GROUP OF PEOPLE. They
                are the FATHERS and MOTHERS of the
                CHILDREN. Every FATHER and MOTHER
                hug their CHILDREN: both, the war
                protestors and military men.)

                              (ALL WAR PROTESTORS,
                              SOLDIERS and EXTRAS
                              Exit,        laughing
                              joyfully   and    in
                              tender  warmth  with
                              their      PARENTS'
                              embraces.)

                (YOUNG    FAUST,    FATHER,    MOTHER,
           BROTHER return to center stage.)

                         YOUNG FAUST
                      (To his FATHER.)
Dad, how's my dog, Brownie.

                       FAUST'S FATHER
Like I said, alive, but old. He barely gets around.

                       FAUST'S BROTHER
I think you should take him to the vet tomorrow.

                         YOUNG FAUST
For a check-up?

                       FAUST'S BROTHER
No. To put him under. That's what you're used to, ain't it?

                              (LIGHTS FADE.)

                              (CURTAINS.)

                              (END OF SCENE 3.)

ACT 3

Scene 4

SETTING:                          FAUST and WAGNER are still
                                  standing to the left side of
                                  the stage witnessing a
                                  reenactment of FAUST'S youth
                                  at his parent's small house.

AT RISE:                          Enter YOUNG FAUST and his
                                  FATHER.


                        YOUNG FAUST
Dad, I couldn't find Brownie in the living room, in the
kitchen, nor in my bedroom. Where is he?


                        FAUST'S FATHER
In the garage.


                        YOUNG FAUST
It's hot in there.


                        FAUST'S FATHER
So? He smells. He's too old and too sick to be in the
house. He's always coughing up and vomiting. Your mother's
tired of cleaning up after your dog. Why he's still around
is a mystery to me.


                        YOUNG FAUST
So, he should be dead like me. Save you guys a bunch of
embarrassing things.


                        FAUST'S FATHER
You read that in my words? If you're going to quarrel with
me, maybe you should stay at someone else's house.


                        YOUNG FAUST
I'm not arguing with you. I just want to see my dog.
                    (YOUNG FAUST bolts into the garage.
                    He returns a few seconds later
                    carrying BROWNIE in his arms.)
Dad, it's too hot in the garage for him. He's staying with
me.

> (Exit FAUST'S FATHER.)

YOUNG FAUST [CON'T]
> (Stage light only on him.)

Hey fellow. I miss you. I miss you so much. You're the only one I ever loved.

> (BROWNIE becomes motionless.)

Hear me, doggie? I love you.

> (YOUNG FAUST, realizing his dog died in his arms, breaks out crying.)

> (Enter FAUST'S MOTHER. Stage lights brighten throughout the stage.)

FAUST'S MOTHER
Better take him to the vet. They'll dispose of his body.

YOUNG FAUST
Dispose of his body? Why not wrap him in a body bag and place a flag over him and play taps? What is wrong with you, mother? What is wrong with you?

FAUST'S MOTHER
Don't talk to me like that!

YOUNG FAUST
I'm sorry, mother. I'm sorry. But I'm not taking Brownie to any vet. I'm burying him in the backyard.

FAUST'S MOTHER
Oh, no, you're not. That's a filthy thing to do. He'll stink up the whole neighborhood.

YOUNG FAUST
Don't worry. I'll bury him deep. With his burial I'll bury my own soul. The devil can have it for all I care.

> (Enter RACHAEL.)

RACHAEL
Faust, rewind a third time. Let go of your anger. It still haunts you. Think before you speak.

(Stage lights dim. Red light on
RACHAEL, green light on FAUST.)

                    YOUNG FAUST
Don't worry, mom. I'll bury him deep. And, who knows,
perhaps in a few years, after I get married, have a house,
I'll find another dog with Brownie's qualities.

                              (ALL EXIT.)

(Stage lights dim. Then suddenly
come back on at full intensity.))

                                   (Enter YOUNG FAUST,
                                   running to center
                                   stage with a shovel
                                   in his hand.
                                   Furiously, he slams
                                   the shovel into the
                                   stage.)

                    YOUNG FAUST
                 (A spontaneous,
          horrific scream fills the stage,
                 crying intensely.)
NO! NO! NO! I didn't want to hurt anyone! But they wanted
to hurt me. To kill me. To kill my friends. NO! NO! NO! To
hell with everyone. I'll worship and serve only him who
really understands this world.

          (Doubles down in anguish.)

                              (Enter RACHAEL.)

Faust, rewind a fourth time. Then a fifth time, and onward,
until you have taken back all your pledges. On each rewind,
be careful with your new words.

          (Stage lights dim.)

                                   (Exit RACHAEL and
                                   YOUNG FAUST.)

                                   (Re-enter YOUNG
                                   FAUST.)

                         YOUNG FAUST
                      (A spontaneous,
                   crying fills the stage.)
Mom, Dad, I apologize for my behavior. I don't know how to
act, what to say, how to behave. Please, allow me some time
to readjust, to relearn where I'm at and how I should
proceed. Please, forgive me.
                      (Lights  Fade.  YOUNG  FAUST  moves
                      toward his older self, and both face
                      other.)
I am reconciled.


                      (YOUNG FAUST steps behind his older
                      self into the darker part of the
                      stage. FASUT follows his movement.
                      He lifts his hand halfway toward his
                      younger self, then looks at his hand
                      as  tears  begin  to  flow  down  his
                      cheeks.)


                         FAUST
                   (Repeats his younger version's words.
I am reconciled.


                                   (LIGHTS FADE.)

                                   (CURTAINS.)

                                   (END OF SCENE 4.)

ACT 3

Scene 5

SETTING:                    Play enters present time.

AT RISE:                    Stage lights brighten again,
                            showing only "aged" FAUST
                            sitting on a chair, his head
                            resting in his arms.)


                    FAUST
        (Speaks with a poetic tone.)

*O sad, embittered world,*
*Why is your soul filled with such distress?*
*Is there no end to your anxiety?*
*Anxiously you demand finalization.*

*What am I to do?*
*Oh, these images . . .*
*these ravaging images*
      *will they never leave me alone?*

*What am I to do?*
*Where exists my joyful myrrh?*
*Oh dread, dread, leave me alone!*
      *Leave me alone.*
*My virtue is snapped.*
      *Veritas, you are such a joke.*

*What am I to do?*
  *Surrender? Not I. Never, I.*

*What am I to do.*
  *I can surge forward. Surge!*
  *Climb to the top of Mount Everest!*
  *For I am I, and what I am, I am.*
  *And I, being I, shall climb*
    *to the top of*
        *Mount Everest!*

        (FAUST collapses to the floor,
        loudly moaning, his hands cross in
        front of his chest.)

                                        (MARGARET      rushes
                                        onto     the    stage,
                                        flinging      herself
                                        beside her husband's
                                        shivering body.)

                          MARGARET
                (Crying desperately as she
                 immediately embraces FAUST.)
Faust. What happened? What happened? I'll call an
ambulance.


                           FAUST
Margaret . . . what am I to do? Oh, God, let me die so I
can see the world from atop Mount Everest, and there, stomp
this world's bitterness away, finding within . . . joy.
Margaret, this is the perfect time for me to die. My soul
has been purchased by God.


                          MARGARET
Die? You? A man more than a man. Tell me . . . what
happened to make you so despondent?


                           FAUST
My parents killed my dog. They killed Brownie.
                    (He gets up and rushes to the center
                     of the stage, staring directly at
                     the audience.)
My parents . . . my brother . . . my best friend . . . all
of this damnable society . . . they killed Brownie. The
only love I ever had.
                    (He wails loudly, folding over as he
                     tightens his fists.)
OW! I hurt. MARGARET. I hurt. The pain is intolerable.
                    (MARGARET rushes to him and wraps
                     him inside her arms. Suddenly, he
                     breaks from her arms, shouting.)
WAGNER! WAGNER!
Why did you have to die?
                    (Pauses, his hands lifting up toward
                     the audience, away from MARGARET.)
Michael . . . I'm so sorry.
                    (FAUST drops his arms to a neutral
                     position as she hugs him tighter to
                     her chest. With renewed strength, he
                     gets  up,  walks  closer  to  the
                     audience.)

AMERICA!

>(FAUST lifts his arms, arches his
>back as he faces the audience. He
>begins a dance-like movement,
>pauses, then shouts triumphantly.)

*LOS ESTADOS UNIDOS es siempre mi casa*!

>(Turns to MARGARET. He holds out
>his hand to her. She rushes to him
>and embraces him tightly.)

Margaret, Margaret, I love you. I love you. I, I . . .
love . . . America. My home, *mi casa, es siempre . . .
siempre . . . siempre . . .* America.

>(Pauses. MARGARET kisses him.)

Margaret, I am no longer despondent.

>(FAUST grasps at his heart as he
>collapses, his hand stretched away
>from his body. Dies.)

MARGARET

>(Falls on her knees, sobbing,
>then lifts her hands toward the ceiling.)

Heavenly Father, Yehuway, sacred is Your name.
I pledge allegiance to your eternal kingdom.
Your laws and judgments are supreme over everything.

>(MARGARET walks over to the sofa
>table and picks up the statue of La
>Negrita and shouts.)

Oh, mother of God, he was your son, just like he was my
husband. Remember him with all your love, just as I have
loved him with all my love.

>(LIGHTS FADE.)

>(CURTAINS.)

>(END OF SCENE 4.)

ACT 4

Scene 1

SETTING:                              FAUST    stands    in    front    of
                                      RACHAEL'S House with a bag of
                                      prime dog biscuits.

AT RISE:                              Enter RACHAEL with REGIS tied
                                      to a leash.


                          RACHAEL
I just came from your house. You really like disturbing
your neighbors, don't you. All that drama. Was it really
necessary?

                           FAUST
Only for me. The wind of gentleness has long ago ceased to
cool me from my violent rages.

                          RACHAEL
Didn't I comfort your soul?

                           FAUST
Yes. Tell me, can everyone on earth rewind and undo their
mistakes?

                          RACHAEL
Yes.

                           FAUST
Who are you?

                          RACHAEL
I am she who has long watched over you since the day your
mother prayed for you in the Basilica of Our Lady of the
Angels when the volcano, Irazu, blew up, destroying your
village, killing all its residents, that is, except for
you. . . . Then, Margaret repeated your mother's same
prayer, which your mother taught to her, when you learned
of Wagner's death. Your prayer, I also heard.

                         FAUST
It was spoken in a moment of weakness and fear. I wished I
had died during the Battle of An Loc. I would have been so
much more useful: feeding the maggots.
                    (Pauses. Looks at RACHAEL.)
You said the Basilica of Cartago, Costa Rica. You once said
to me that a friend of yours sent you to me. Is she Costa
Rica's patron saint?


                         RACHAEL
I am she. Time and distance mean nothing to me.


                         FAUST
You are La Negrita, the patron saint of Costa Rica?


                         RACHAEL
I am the mother of all races, of all nationalities. In
Costa Rica, I chose a young mestiza girl, Juana Pereira, to
come upon me to declare to the world my purpose. In France
I chose another, and in Portugal another yet, and in
Mexico, still another.


                         FAUST
So that's why you can say to me that you know everything
about me.


                         RACHAEL
Yes. Everything.


                         FAUST
Even what has long plagued me?


                         RACHAEL
Yes, I know of your harboring guilt over your survival
through so many battles and the guilt, that has plagued you
through the last five decades, of what you did to Michael,
your friend.


                         FAUST
I've always wondered why nothing ever seemed able to take
me down. All the bullets missing me. All the dark alleys
free from strife and from danger.
                    (FAUST  motions  as  if  a  stealth
                    fighter.)
Even when I fought hand-to-hand, it was as though I knew
exactly where to position my body: when to dodge, when to
sidestep. Slow motion in severe reality.

                    (Resumes normal stance.)
And, yes, it is true. Michael was my friend. He was the
only soldier in Pleiku who never saw me as a Hispanic.
Never treated me less than what I am. He not only obeyed
all my commands, he executed them thoroughly. Charismatic,
handsome, fun, Michael whom I beat up so severely, he ended
up in the hospital for three days. He whose right eye I
gouged out.


                         RACHAEL
Finish your confession.


                         FAUST
Charismatic, white, gay Michael one morning asked me to
lend him ten dollars to have sex with a prostitute to prove
to himself he was a man, not a queer. Naturally, I lent it
to him . . . but the weeks dragged by without him paying me
back the ten dollars. The men in my unit began calling me a
punk-ass coward, a homo-lover. A 'Mex' officer with
multiple kills who was too afraid to get back from a "soft"
white man ten miserable dollars. Despite my rank, despite
that Michael was under my command, despite my friendship, I
relented to the degrading name-calling and disrespect. On a
morning of agitated disgrace, I confronted Michael . . .
charming, gay Michael . . . and beat him with all the power
that I could muster from within myself. After I plummeted
and bloodied him, I took from his wallet what belonged to
me. Ten fuckin' dollars.


                         RACHAEL
What did you do with the money you took back from him?


                         FAUST
                    (Starting to cry.)
I visited that same whore house that Michael liked so much.
I took all my men with me and bought a hundred beers at ten
cents each. When I became fully drunk and uncaring, I took
his woman twice over. Long, long afterward, I cried like a
miserable drunkard when Michael lost his right eye on
account of my beating. Rachael, or angel, or whatever you
are, what ever happened to Michael?


                         RACHAEL
He became a heroin addict and an alcoholic. He tried
detoxing in Japan before he got out of the Army, but it
didn't work. He remained a drug user until he died. He
never recovered from his loss of dignity, from the loss of

his eye, suffering not from an enemy's assault, but from a
vicious assault by his most trusted friend. He died lonely.
Destitute. Yet, in the end, he forgave you.

FAUST

How I wish I had never taken those horrid ten dollars, not
beaten him up, not taken away from him, his sight.

RACHAEL

But you made up for it, giving away money to anyone who
asked you for it, never once asking for the money to be
paid back to you. Helping people with their houses:
painting them for free, doing electrical and plumbing work
for free. Cutting their grass whenever they asked. Talking
and consoling them with their troubles. A person's sinful
reaction to harshness becomes and remains their guilt. You
prayed for forgiveness, and you received forgiveness. God
tested your repentance many times over. Don't worry.
Michael forgave you for he never lost his love for you.

FAUST

What becomes of me, now that I am dead?

RACHAEL

Margaret's prayer has been answered. Yours as well. Here,
take Regis' leash in your hand. Old Regis will lead you
anywhere you want to go.

FAUST

Heaven?

RACHAEL

If you want it, it's open to you. Michael is waiting for
you as are your parents.

FAUST

And Wagner?

RACHAEL

He died before I could save him. A wager was made in heaven
between the demon and God about your soul, so Wagner was
permitted to visit you, and, if you repented, he will be
given an opportunity to reside in a world far better than
Tartarus.

FAUST

And, Margaret, will she be in heaven for me?

                    RACHAEL
Margaret will soon be there.

                     FAUST
And those whom I harmed?

                    RACHAEL
All will receive you with arms filled with love . . . with
treasured forgiveness.

                     FAUST
My generation had Vietnam. Today's generation has Iran.
Tomorrow's generation will have nothing but radiated
sawdust. Though debts can be discharged, obligations can
never be erased. In the eyes of the multitude of gods and
beliefs, everyone fought for what they believed was right.
Only in the finalization of all things will we be able to
understand and know what is right and what is truth. When
all these notions come to bear in comparison, only then, in
peace, will the substance of our souls—the being of our
essence—find salvation.

                              (LIGHTS FADE.)

                              (CURTAINS.)

                              (END OF PLAY.)

www.ingramcontent.com/pod-product-compliance
Lightning Source LLC
Chambersburg PA
CBHW060204120726
48004CB00007B/1687